We Are Enough

A Carnegie Writers Publication

Program Facilitators

Flor Abarca | Kemi Elufiede | Lillian Olney

Carnegie Kids Club Authors

Corbin Bell | Ashlynn Boucher | Sunny Caldwell | Hiyab K. Dawit
Ayla Hardy | Ezra Heggem | Hollis Herlocker | Charlotte Ingles
Makayla Kendall | Caden Kie | Reginald Pearson
Aayden Polard | Joey Rueckert | Blake Swift | Samira Weaver

Teen Authors

Briana Beel | Heidy Canales | Jonnyka Carter | Alyson Cordova
Savannah Dunigan | Asael Garcia | Cameron Hudson
Braelyn Jones | William Mathis-Dixon | Joy Nuñez
Emanuel Pimental-Aguirre | Jan Michael Robinson
Victoria Santiago | Sandro Zavala

We Are Enough
Published by Carnegie Writers, Inc.
Prepared for Publication by Carissa Barker-Stucky
Copyright 2026 © Carnegie Writers, Inc.

ISBN: 979-8-9923614-4-5 (print)
ISBN: 979-8-9923614-5-2 (ebook)

For permissions contact: publications@carnegiewriters.com

TABLE OF CONTENTS

From The
Carnegie
Kids Club

Strong Foundations for Fulfilling Dreams

Carnegie Kids Club aims to guide the youngest creatives among us by improving literacy skills through reading, writing, and art. Elementary students in our After-School Program learn about the basics of creative writing and storytelling while incorporating movement exercises to help both mind and body grow. For this anthology, participants turned in self-reflection poems, collaborative tales written as a team, and a comic book adventure.

Let's learn a little bit about this year's students:

Ashlynn Boucher

I enjoy watching and playing hockey. I like doing cartwheels, splits, back-bends, etc. I love hanging out with good family and friends. I would say I am outgoing, kind, friendly, a leader, and ambitious. Some qualities I have are making friends and not caring what people think about me. In the future, I want to learn another language, learn new skills, and make new friends. One interesting thing about me is that I am great at math.

SUNNY CALDWELL
My name is Sunny Caldwell, and I'm in the fifth grade. I like drawing, playing basketball, and soccer. I am funny and creative. In the future, I hope to be very successful at being a comedian. Fun fact about me is I am good at creating dialogue.

HIYAB K. DAWIT
Hello fellow readers, my name is Hiyab. I am in 4th grade. I enjoy my time making comic books, and I like reading. I am a good tickler, got it? In the future, I will be an author.

Thanks for reading.

Hollis Herlocker

My name is Hollis. I have a friend named Maria. I had a cat named Walter who passed. I am in good health; I also sell pencils. I am good at making things, and I can engineer well. That's probably it.

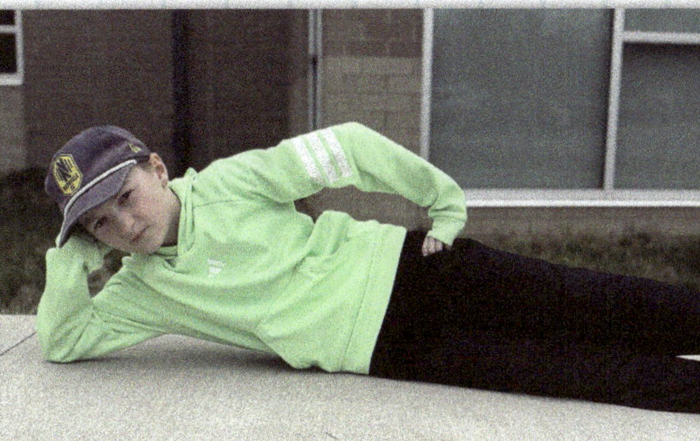

Ezra Heggem

Hi, my name is Ezra and I'm in the fifth grade. I love to play games like *Hollow Knight* and stuff like that. I like pizza and ELA class at school. I am good at video games and soccer. I would love to be a video game developer. Something important about me is being good at math.

Charlotte Ingles

My name is Charlotte, and I am in the 4th grade. A few things I enjoy are reading, drawing, and writing history. I am good at reading and love trying new things. In the future, I hope to become a teacher, librarian, or an author.

Makayla Kendall

Hello, my name is Makayla. I am a fifth grader! My hobbies are drawing, writing, and playing soccer. My favorite subjects are English and art. I'm creative and have a weird laugh that I adore. I am always willing to try new food, because I love food. My dream is to become a popular artist. One interesting thing about me is I can speak Japanese.

Caden Kie

Hello, my name is Caden, and I'm in fourth grade. I like to play football with my friends. I am a good listener. In the future, I hope to be a football player in the NFL. Something important is being with my family.

REGINALD PEARSON
Hi, my name is Reginald; I am in fifth grade. I like to do art, and my favorite hobby is making stuff from cardboard such as swords. I like football. I am good at basketball. I would describe myself as funny. In the future I would like to play in the NBA.

JOEY RUECKERT
Hello, my name is Joey; I am in the fourth grade. I love to draw and make up characters, I am creative and imaginative. In the future, I hope to become a theme park owner. One interesting thing about me is I am silly.

BLAKE SWIFT

My name is Blake, and I am in the fifth grade. I enjoy soccer and basketball. I am athletic and good at math. I want to be a basketball player when I grow up. I am school greeter and ambassador.

SAMIRA WEAVER

Hi, my name is Samira, and I'm in fourth grade. My hobby is playing at the park. I have a quirky and kind personality, and when I grow up I want to be a police officer. One thing about me is that I have great facial expressions. Also, I have a dog that is a mix of a pitbull and a Labrador.

Reflections Through Poetry

I AM

One of the many uses for creative writing is self-reflection and growth. During a poetry exercise, students were encouraged to write about themselves— who they are, who they wish to be, what they like about themselves.

I Am Ashlynn

I am growing into someone who can walk in their own shoes
Someone who loves who they are
I have enough confidence to build a house
I am proud of me because I am kind
Not only with my personality but with my actions
Enough kindness to share with the world
Me heart is filled with confidence
The kind where I love myself

I Am Ayla

I am kind
With my body and my mind.
I don't doubt
I try to think about these things.
But something...
Something makes me think it's not enough.
Everyone tells me I am enough, but...
Something makes me think I can't —
But now, I am starting to make a change.
I know I can.
I *am* enough!

I Am Hollis

I am someone who can make stuff out of nothing
I love the engineer in me
I love to build

I Am Blake

I am good at basketball
I feel confident when I play basketball
Nobody can tell me otherwise
I am proud of myself when I play
No one can put me down

I Am Samira

I am someone who loves me
I love the part of me that loves others
My heart is full of love

Collaborative Writing

The following stories were written by our young authors working together in groups. Collaborative Writing exercises help introduce concepts of storytelling while also encouraging partnership between students, inspiring growth in their creative and academic futures. Students spin marvelous tales while learning to work as a team.

The Dig Site

Collaborative Story Excerpt
Written by Ayla and Reginald

Once upon a time, two researchers named Reginald and Ayla were walking home after a long day of work at a dig site at an Egyptian Pyramid, where they found pieces of ancient gold. They were taking a short cut through ancient ruins because they were very tired. Suddenly, Ayla stepped on something out of place— a shiny metal piece with writing in an ancient language. The young researchers looked at the metal; it said "Hyperpalateleportation." The pair were stumped and decided to take it back with them to the home lab.

A few steps later, Reginald stepped on another metal piece! This one said "Anthropomorphiicatalatale." The pieces looked like they would fit perfectly with one another. It was very late, so Reginald and Ayla decided to investigate it tomorrow.

The next day, the two researchers went back to the ruins— there were more pieces! They started collecting all the pieces and putting them together. The metal pieces started glowing, and far away, they could see another piece glowing in response. They sprinted towards it and grabbed the last piece at the same time. This one said "Destinoationhybeshmoishealigestic." With the last piece found, an ancient button rose from the sand. Next to the button was a sign that said "Don't push." Unfortunately, part of it was faded! The researchers thought it said "Push." After pushing the button, Reginald and Ayla heard a mystical voice say, "Teleportation system activating…" The pieces were a teleportation charm! As the researchers levitated into a futuristic horse pirate ship that was completely empty, they couldn't help but wonder where they would go next… outside of the ship, Reginald and Ayla could now hear dinosaurs howling. They had gone back in time!

The magical glow from the teleportation charm came back, and the pair were sent to different places. Reginald became a saber-tooth tiger, and Ayla became a little saber-tooth fox. Where could they have gone?

To Be Continued...

Mermaid Fable

Collaborative Short Story
Written by Ashlynn, Ayla, and Reginald

Once upon a time, on one fateful day, a mermaid princess who was very full of herself felt like she was too good for her home. Since she was bored, she decided to leave the other mermaids and explore past her boundaries. The mermaid princess was used to getting whatever she wanted from her dad, so she decided to leave without telling the others.

Some sunken treasure caught her eye. She had never seen real treasure before, so she decided to go after it to take it for herself. Suddenly, a strong current formed— she couldn't pull herself against it! The mermaid couldn't help but remember when her father, the king of the mermaids, told her to practice swimming and she didn't. While the current swept her away, the mermaid wished she had practiced. She was swept past a sailor's boat, a dock, and a beach full of people! She didn't know where she ended up... the mermaid was lost in the ocean.

The sailors on the boat she passed started singing sea shanties, so the mermaid followed the noise. On her way to the boat, she saw her father. She was saved! The king of the mermaids took his spoiled-princess daughter back to the mermaid kingdom and told her to never leave alone again. The next day, the mermaid practiced her swimming.

The End!

20

My Future is Golden

Collaborative Poem
Written by Ashlynn and Reginald

Being a kid is no fun,
Every single day I must go to school,
And after— I have a bedtime,
While the adults get to play in the sun.

If I was older, I would drive a car,
I would go anywhere in the world that I want,
Right down the street to my friend's house,
But I'm scared I would get trapped in tar.

When I am grown, I will have a phone,
Every single day I will text my homies,
I will grow tall— I will have bigger bones,
And then I will open my mailbox to all the loans.

CLARK THE SHARK

Collaborative Poem
Written by Aayden, Ashlynn, Ayla, Blake,
Caden, Corbin, Ezra, Hiyab, Hollis, Joey,
Makayla, Reginald, Samira, and Sunny.

The capybara was a lazy guy,
I saw a man eating my crispy fly,
the capybara spends his time watching flies,
the guy always lies.

Even though he's a weird guy,
his name was Mozy and he was always very cozy,
his daughter was named Rozy,
his girlfriend is called Cozy.

I saw someone that was cooking with a stove,
Mozy's toesies got eaten by crowsies,
his sticky nose-y got a little posy,
he also likes to eat posies.

The toesies play football,
Messi is better than Ronaldo,
Clark the shark ate some bark,
now the baby doll wants to go to the park.

The baby doll was asleep
because it had too much energy,
baby doll also got eaten by Clark (the shark),
the baby doll liked toes,
I like bark.

The dragon likes Halloween,
the dragon later bought a wagon,
the dragon tried to eat the Cheez-it,
but, the Cheez-it said "beat it!"

Clark the shark has returned,
now Clark has to go to school and learn,
but when he tried to learn, he got burned,
Clark got mad, so he ate the paper.

After a few days, Clark found a painter,
but the painter said "beat it!" and ran away,
Clark the shark decided to have war
with the Cheez-it,
Clark the shark wants to have more Cheez-its!

Clark the shark ate Stunk the monk,
then hit the wall with a very big *thunk*,
then Clark the shark said "RAWR,"
then Clark the shark made a mistake
and turned into Clark ate bark.

CLARK THE SHARK IS THE GOAT.

Aliens at Sayam's Club

Collaborative Playwriting Excerpt
Written by Aayden, Ashlynn, Ayla, Blake,
Charlotte, Caden, Corbin, Ezra, Hiyab,
Joey, Makayla, Samira, and Sunny.

Character List:

Chicken Fillet Driver, an alien hunter
Fred, an alien
Bob, an alien
Isabella Diane Bethabelle, a spoiled girl who is
prisoner to the aliens
Green-er, an alien
Wesley, a co-owner
Mr. Smelly, founder of the Sayam's Club
Bluu, a dog that can become blue
Frank, just some guy
Frank the Third, an apocalyptic survivor from the
aliens
Thing 67, six seveeeen
Abacah, a green child
Dr. Nefarious, an evil alien doctor and inventor
Violet, a jellyfish that can turn into a girl

Summary:

Abacah, Bob, and Fred try burning a Sayam's
Club to ashes, but Bob betrays Fred and locks
him in a closet— he is burned to ashes! The

24

green alien betrays Fred and slaps him in the face and kills him. Then, Frank looks at the scene and tries to run away but gets abducted by the aliens.

Violet the jellyfish looks at the world, and Dr. Nefarious takes it over. Bluu, the dog that becomes blue, takes over the world second. Isabella Diane Bethabelle gets released from the aliens and becomes president of the world.

[Scene One: FRED, BOB, and FRANK THE THIRD are in Sayam's Club. FRED and BOB are undercover and working as Sayam's Club employees. FRANK THE THIRD is at FRED and BOB's checkout till.]

FRANK THE THIRD
I want to see all of your comic books!
Where are they?

FRED
Comics are in aisle 2…or aisle 6— I'm
new, so I don't really know.

BOB
We are in training.

FRANK THE THIRD
Okay… thank you for the information,
weirdos. I will go walk myself over there
now.

BOB
Hey! That is not very kind.

FRED and BOB laugh… he is falling right into their trap! FRANK THE THIRD begins walking.

FRANK THE THIRD
No comics here… those dumb
employees don't even know their store.
Maybe they are down this bottomless
pit at the end of the aisle?

FRANK THE THIRD takes the ladder into the hole.

FRED and BOB
Bahahaha you have fallen right into our
trap! Now we can abduct you with our
giant alien spaceship with millions of
aliens inside it… mwahaha!

FRED and BOB's laughter devolves into coughing.

FRANK THE THIRD
Is this a prank?

FRED
No.

FRANK THE THIRD
Well… there's nothing else I can do… I
guess I should just give up.

FRED and BOB
AHHHHHHH! WE ARE ALLERGIC TO
PEOPLE GIVING UP!

FRED and BOB run away screaming.

FRANK THE THIRD
Ha! Those stupid employees… I mean
aliens. They are allergic to the dumbest
thing!

[FRANK THE THIRD takes FRED and BOB's alien
supplies and starts chasing after them.]

To Be Continued...

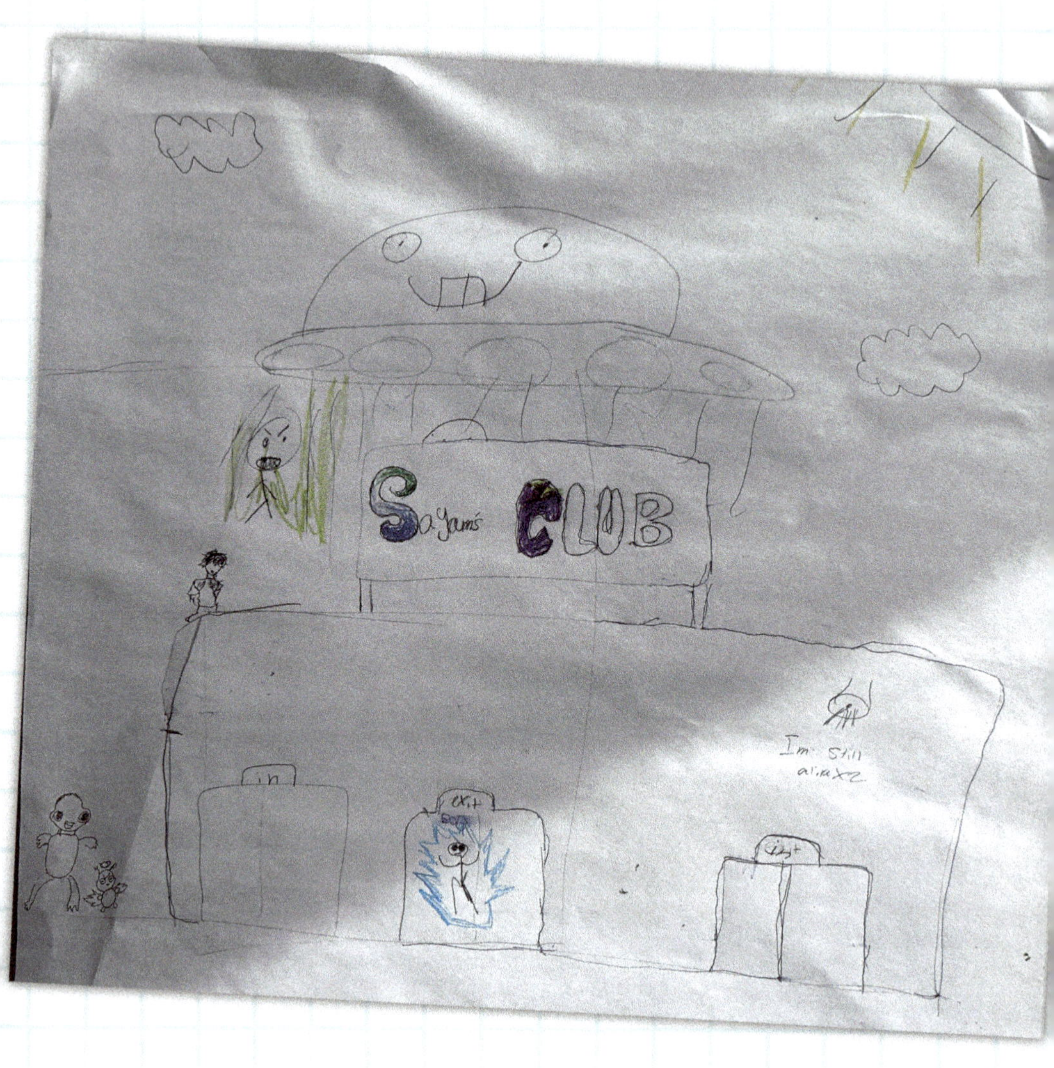

28

STUFF ABOUT FOOTBALL

Collaborative Article Writing
Written by Aayden, Ashlynn, Ayla, Blake,
Caden, Hiyab, Hollis, Joey, Makayla,
Samira, and Sunny.

Football is a very popular sport in the United States. Football starts with a ball and an end zone. The ball is brown, and it has white stripes on it— and it has 16 lace holes with 8 cross stitches. The Giants played the Bears, and the Bears caught a headtop, and then the quarterback threw a whole entire spiral. The Vanderbilt Commodores played the LSU Tigers, and they cooked so much and won.

Football is good for lots of different people because there are so many different positions: you can block, you can tackle people— it's not all the same! Football can be used to get your anger out. Football players wear special gear to keep themselves safe when they play. In the United States, each state has a different team. Sometimes there are multiple, because of the SEC and the NFL. In Hispanic countries, football is the name for soccer.

The War of Planet X
The War Between the Chickens and the Humans

Collaborative Short Story
Written by Aayden, Ashlyn, Ayla, Charlotte, Corbin, Ezra, Hiyab, Hollis, Joey, Makayla, Reginald, Samira, and Sunny.

An astronaut goes into space and hits an asteroid that is orbiting a planet. This planet was an unidentified one called Planet X; this astronaut was sent out to investigate it. As he got closer in his rocket, he saw a bunch of aliens and named the planet 'Planet Alien'. The astronaut was hesitant because he knew he was not the first one sent out— another astronaut had investigated before and never came back. After the astronaut hit the asteroid, his rocket crashed and landed in some sort of goo. He couldn't get his ship out. While no one on Earth knew where the astronaut went, the astronaut was found by alien chickens. His astronaut helmet had fallen off in the crash— he had no oxygen! The chicken aliens took the astronaut captive and put him in an oxygen chamber...where he met the alien chicken princess. The aliens ran tests on him and told him he is half human and half alien chicken.

No one knew that he was followed by a dragon, who wanted to break him out! The dragon roasted all the chicken aliens and turned them into fried chicken. While the astronaut was enjoying his life on Earth, the chickens were working on getting the spaceship out of the goo. They built their own ships, as well, and followed the astronaut and the dragon back to Earth. The chickens said, "Ahh… at last we are finally on Planet E! WE ARE GOING TO DESTROY THE HUMANS AND TAKE OVER THE EARTH!" It turns out there were some blue aliens spying on them, and they decided to help the humans! They shot missiles at the alien chicken ship; the astronaut shot another missile that destroyed the chicken aliens. But… there was one left! All the other chickens got fried in a frying pan; the humans ate the alien chickens and said, "Wow, this is delicious! We want more of this."

Surprise! The chickens called for reinforcements before they were eaten— the chickens were back! The chicken aliens were in a war with the humans. One chicken said, "Don't eat us, and we won't fight you." Then they became friends.

The End

Planet X

Language and Imagery

Words are not the only way to express oneself. We also encourage students to explore various forms of artwork, from illustrations to go along with their stories to blackout poetry. This year, we even had students come together to create a comic book.

Blackout Poetry

Created by Reginald

Things I Like about Me

~~I like the texture of oil pastels,~~
~~...fingers,~~
~~the sensation of drawing~~
~~...~~
~~...cozy feeling~~
~~of drawing eye after eye~~ 

~~I love the even back and forth~~
~~of swinging on my swing set~~
~~and the way it makes my mind fly.~~
~~I love~~ the oily smell ~~of Pop's basement~~
~~makes my brain smile from talking~~ with Pop
~~about trains and myths~~
~~and how to~~ build ~~something from scratch~~
charges ~~...~~

~~How the familiar~~ sound
~~of the~~ *Lord of the Ring* ~~soundtrack~~
every time ~~...~~ (I?)
~~watch the movies together at her house~~
~~and the calming sound~~
~~of Mrs. V's voice~~
~~in the ... of English class~~

~~Sometimes I click my~~ teeth
~~even though my dentist says I shouldn't~~
~~because my jaw likes to move~~
~~to the rhythm of songs~~
~~and chew on ice.~~

~~Sometimes I blink real hard~~
~~or squeeze my hands into fists~~
~~or scribble in my notebook~~
~~when the feelings inside me~~
~~are too big for words. I love~~ the way
~~feelings pump through~~
~~my whole body like~~ blood,

~~how ... my~~
~~from everything,~~ I feel.

~~Sometimes I jump~~
~~feeling~~
~~Sometimes ...~~ gotta jump.

Fingerprint Poetry

Ark lark
HOMSSSS bugerson
Alt Cabawt Sembus intolig
RATsickle Flimbus
Qviz
bagsimon
ratcon
Harhhiba
bialholigy rat aboliton
Simlic
Parmriz
Simbly abebe

38

Hello my name is
I Like ART
My favorite co I have tons of I have one Brother
older si! o Spring
I love to Draw I want to be an Artist when
I have cousins
I have a messy laugh I Bea ear root Beer
I Love ANIMALS
I Love nature
I Do not like Bugs (At least most of them)
I have one Dog and one cat
I am learning Spanish
I Am creative I want to go to college I love to draw
I'm Learning how to knit I love stories I love Baking I am cool
I Like writing
I ♥ FOOD Specifically PASTA
SAVE THE TREES
I Like Astronomy
My Mom Hasan
I Like Reading
I Like fiction I go camping
I Luv Books

Hollis

bibliphobia
Larry birds
Simso
baggerton cobalt Linus
arrest hombass
flimbusechem
phavnimonapia
bimbo bic simtics
Sharpie alt
elinstin
Gelliteio
solo ssart harboi
ratopolotein

40

Hello, my name is Charlotte. I love Art, Reading, and E.L.A. I have a really cool school and Amazing friends. My favirote color is Green. One of my nicknames is Char. I am a creative and silly person. I do well in school and try my best in all my classes. Three of my faviorte subjects are history, ELA and science. I am a very colorful person and love cats and dogs and bunnies. I have 4 animals at home. I also love writing and history books. And I want to be a teacher when I grow up. I also enjoy baking. I want to be able to knit soon. I want

41

name is makayla! ♡

I dont have a weird laugh! ☺

When I was young I was doing horbly Push ups

I started drowing when I was 2 years old Also my drawings are cool!

I like ramen and root beer! I have around Two pounds of rice

Also im obsessed with stars. I have or most of my stuff has stars!

I like cats and dogs ovny animal really. I like insects! Also spiders.

I have a phobia of something to do with heights? I watch anime!

My favrite anime is demon slayer plus character is shinobu and Tomayo

My favirote hoiday is holloween! Because I like scary and sweet costume

I manly use chop sticks. its like everything to me

I am great at eating. Also

Hi my name is Reginald.
my faviort color is BLUE.
favirote thing to do is art
and i Like to say is
that my faviort pictures work
my faviorte plante is Saturn
faviorte sone is from Jin ieko.
and my

43

44

45

Unstoppables Blast Off In Space

Comic by Hiyab and Joey

Top: One time, Hiyab and Fwed were thinking about something to do.
p3. Hiyab: "Let's go to the NASA space place!"
p4. And so...
p5. Scientist: "Hello! Want to see our rocket? It's almost done!"
p6. Hiyab: "Fine with me!" | Fwed: "Sure."
p7. Hiyab: "Something feels wrong. Should we go?" | Fred: "Quiet, Hiyab, he's probably a fan." | Hiyab: "Okay, okay."
p8. Fred: "Whoa, these are awesome!" | Hiyab: "Yeah, but they're expensive!"
p9. **Slam**!
p10. Hiyab: "Hey, open the door! If you press a green button, it will work."
p11. Fwed: "Maybe this one?"
p12. **RUMBLE** | Fwed: "That's not good!" | Hiyab: "We'd better buckle up!"

Top 3: *RUMBLE | FWOOSH | FWOOSH*

p5. Person 1: "I didn't know there was a launch." | Person 2: "Me neither."

p6. Fred: "Are you okay?" | Hiyab: "Yeah."

p7. Hiyab: "Hey, what's that?"

p8. Khan: "My name is Federal Agent Khan Emma, but you may call me Commander Khan."

p9. Khan: "The US Space Force wants you heroes to get five items from outer space."

p1. Khan: "We need to find an ancient tablet, a rare gem, a powerful orb, a magical cube, and a hat."
p2. Hiyab: "A hat?"
p3. Khan: "I ran out of objectives."
p4. Hiyab: "Can you give us a moment?"
p5. Hiyab: "I told you something was wrong!" | Fred: "Okay, but can we—" | Hiyab: "No!"
p6. Khan: "If that's how you feel, just press that red button. The choice is yours."
p7. Fred: "Wait!"
p8. Hiyab: "You want to stay?"
p9. Fwed: "After all you said, I understand. But since we are already up here, we might as well do it, right?"

p1-2. Hiyab: "Hmmm...sure." | Fwed: "Yay!"
p3. Fwed: "Yeah!" | Hiyab: "Grr, I'm very angry at you, Fwed." | Khan: "Ok, buckle up!"
p4. Fwed: "Ummmm...." | *FWOOSH* | Hiyab: "AAAAAH!"

Hiyab: "UNFAIR!"
Fwed: "Hahahaha!"

Top: Meanwhile, back at a secret base.
p1. Octo: "I'll finally stop the Unstoppables!" | Henchman: "Aren't they unstoppable?" | Octo: "Shut up, dummy!"
p2. Octo: "Plus, you're fired." | Henchman: "Heck yaaaaaay!"
p3. Henchman: "Woo-hoo!" | Octo: "Dummy."
p4. Octo: "To space." | *SSHH CRASH*

Top: Meanwhile, back at the mission.
p1. Khan: "First Stop..." | Unstoppables: "Animal World?" | Khan: "Yeah."
p2. Khan: "Animals and a dancing bear live here."
p3. Octo's Ship | Dancing Bear: "HAAAAAAPPY RUN!" | Hiyab: "Wha—" | Fwed: "Ha ha ha ha!"
p4. Fwed: "What the butt?" | Buddy: Gasp

p1. Hiyab: "What-" | Fwed: "-the—"
p2. Buddy: "AAAAAAAAAAAAAH!"
p3. Buddy: "OW—WHOA—AAAAAH!" | Unstoppables: "Uhmmm,,,"
p4. Buddy: "Oh, ok."
p5. Fwed: "What the..." | Buddy: "Super Brother! I'm Buddy."

p1. Hiyab: "What is he doing?" | Buddy: "Huh?" | Fwed: "FOYWE!"
p2. Fwed: "Can we keep him?" | Buddy: "Keep me?"
p3. Hiyab: "NO PETS!" | Buddy: "What's a pet?"

p1. Fwed: "I don't know." | Buddy: Giggle
p2. Hiyab: "Bye, Buddy, we have to find a powerful orb."
p3. Buddy: "The Pith-Orb is that way."
p4. Hiyab: "Okay, you can join us." | Fwed: "Yessss!"

p1. Buddy: "Come on, orb's this way."
p2. Fwed: "What is that?" | Dancing Bear: "Bubbity bub bubbity bub bub!"
p3. Buddy: "There it is, the Pith-Temple."
p4. Hiyab: "Shhh!"
p5. *CLACK* | Buddy: "Ohh, no!"
p6. *SSSSSSS* | Unstoppables: "AHHHH!"

p1. Buddy: "Run!" | Hiyab: "Fly!"
p2. Buddy: "I can't fly, dummies!"
p3. Fwed: "And we can't run!"
p4. Hiyab: "Actually, I can." | Fwed: "Nobody cares!"
p5. Hiyab: "In there!"
p6. Fwed: "Whoa! The place is bigger inside!" | *SLAM* | Buddy/Hiyab: "Whew."
p7. Hiyab: "Whoa!" | Fwed: "The Pith-Orb!"
p8. Buddy: "Wait!" | Fwed: "Hallelujah, Hallelujah!"

p1. *KABOOM KOBOOM*
p2. Unstoppables: "AHHH!"
p3. Buddy: Slap | Hiyab: "Oh snap."
p4. *CRASH*
p5. *FWOOSH* | Octo: "Nooo!"

p1-2. Octo: "Rats! I've lost them again!"
p3. Henchman: "'Sup, Socto." | Octo: "Hey, what are you doing here?...And it's Octo!"
p4. Henchman: "This is my home planet."
p5. Henchman: "See?" | Saowl, Daowl, Mowl, Baowl, Browl.

Octo: "NOOOOOOOO!!!"
Khan: "Let's go to our next stop!"

9

Khan: "Stick-World."
Octo: "I won't lose them this time..."
Stick Penguin

p1. Khan: "Where everyone is a stick figure." | Voice 1; "Uhhh..." | Voice 2: "AHH!"
p2. Stick tree | Fwed: "Whoa, everything is sticks!" | **Rumble** | Hiyab: "I'm starving!" | Buddy: "Same."
p3-4. Hiyab: "Look! A cafe!"
p5. Fwed: "No time to eat, guys."
p6. **Rumble** | Buddy: "You were saying?"

p1. And so, | Hiyab: "Mmmmmm, That was delicious!"
p2. Meanwhile... | Octo: "All right, stay here, y'all. Got it?" | Henchman: "OK, Socto."
p3. Octo: "It's Octo!" | Henchman: "Ooohhh, now I get it! Because you're an octopus."
p4. Henchman: "...Socto." | Octo: "GRRRR!"

p1. **BEEP BEEP**
p2. Octo: "Bye."
p3. Octo: "What is it?" | Voice: "The Unstoppables are near the cafe." | Octo: "Got it."
p4. Octo: "There they are."

p1. Buddy: "What is that?"
p2. Hiyab: "Octo!" | Octo: "Oh, shoot!" | Buddy: "Oct-whatnow?"
p3. Octo: "So long, suckers!" | Hiyab: "Another ship!" | Octo: "But I didn't trap—"
p4. Buddy/Fwed: *What was that?* | Hiyab: "Let's go, guys!"

p1. Buddy: "What-" | Hiyab: "-is-" | Fwed: "-that?" | Sign: King Joey | Stick Monkey Guards
p2. Stick Guard 1: "Pweeeee, owie!" | Stick Guard 2: "Stop right—ow!" | Fwed: "What the Huh?!" | Hiyab: "Are you okay, man?" | Buddy: "Yes." | Stick Guard 2 "Ee-Ee, Oo-Oo, Ah-ah!"
p3-4. King: "Hello, I'm King Joey." | Hiyab: "Hello, King Joey. Is it possible for us to have your hat and gem?" | Buddy/Fwed: "Yeah, please?"

p1. King Joey: "Okay, fine. Only the gem, though." | Hiyab: "Yesss!"
p2. Hiyab: Gulp | King Joey: "Josh Gene!"
p3. Unstoppables: "AHHH!" | Angry Energy | Josh Gene: "I told you never to give anyone the hat OR the gem!"
p4. Josh Gene: "Now I will use the gem against them!"

p1. *FSSSSH* | Unstoppables: "AHHH!"
p2. Hiyab: "I think we should go."

p1. **Snatch** | Josh Gene: "Hey!"

p2. **Snatch** | King Joey: "Not fair!"

p3. Hiyab: "Gem and hat in pocket!" | Super duper angry energy | Josh Gene: "Hey, come back here!" | Unstoppables: "Ahhh!"

p4. **Crash** | Josh Gene: "Come back here!"

p1. Josh Gene: "Noooooooooo!"
p2. Meanwhile... | Octo: "Okay, I've got the location of the Unstoppables..."
p3. Octo: "And I'll destroy them!"
p4. Octo: "Mwahaahaahaahaahaahaahaa!"

Meanwhile...
Swaps
Khan: "Now it's WorldToon!"

p1. Khan: "A Cartoon World—" | Passenger: "D. Duck?" | Duck: "Huh?"
p2-3. Khan: "— where you will find M. Mouse and ask him— | Hiyab: "Can we have the Spin-Tablet?" | Mouse: "Sure!"
p4. Khan: "And bring it back to the ship." | *FSSSSHHHH*

p1. Meanwhile | Henchman: "Are you okay? You've been here for 2 hours." | Octo: "Yeah. I. Am. Fine."
p2. Daowl: "@$#!@$&#" | Henchman: "Should I stay here wit—" | Octo: "NOOOOOOOOO!" | Henchman: "OK."

p1. Khan: "Now it's off to X Game Planet."
p2. *FWOOSH*

16

Khan: "Where games are reality."
Game Glitch side

p1. Khan: "See what I mean?" | Hiyab: "Neat!"
p2. I am Steve, Government | Buddy: "What's that?"
p3. I am Steve, Government
p4. Steve: "Hello, strangers! I am Government Steve!"

p1. Hiyab: "Hello, Steve, Nice to meet you!"
p2. Hiyab: "Hey, guys, it's the cube."
p3. Steve: "They're making me suspicious…" | Hiyab: "See…"
p4. Hiyab: "Please, can we have your cube? Pleeeeease, Steve?!"

p1. Steve: "Oh, heck no! No!" | *BAM*
p2. Hiyab: "Okay."
p3. Ghost: "Stop!" | *Punch* | Steve: "Ugh!" | Buddy: "Dang, man!" | Fwed: "Oooh!"
p4. Hiyab: "Guys, get out!" | Buddy: "Wait, what?" | Ghost: "OoOo!"

p1. Hiyab: "You asked for it! 1-Second Dynamite!"
p2. **BAM** | **FSS** | Hiyab: "Bye!"
p3. **BAA-BOOM** | Voice: "These guys are crazy!" | Buddy: "OMG!" | Hiyab: "Woo-hoo!"
p4. Hiyab: "Ouchie! Oh, shoot!" | **plub** | **Boing**

p2. *Growl*
p4. Octo: "No No No No No No No No No No No No No!!!" | *CRACK CRACK*

p1. **CRACK** | Under...
p2. **CRACK** | **ZZZZZ** | Power supply
p3. **BZZ** | Octo: "NOOOOOO!"
p4. Octo: "That's better.: | **FZ FZ FZ FZ FZ**

p1. On/Off | *POP*
p2. *POP* | Octo: "Huh?"
p3. Peek
p4. Khan: "Since you got all 5 items, you're going back to Earth."

p1. Unstoppables: "Woo-Hoo!"
p2. Khan: "Buckle Up!" | Octo: "Wait, wait!"
p3. *FWOOSH* | Octo: "No fair, man!"
p4. Octo: "Unfair!"

p1. *FWOOSH*
p2. *SSSSS*
p3. *SPLASH*

p2. *GROWL*
p3. *CRASH*

p1. *FZZ*
p2. *FZZ | Growl*
p3. Hiyab: "Uhhh?"
p4. Hiyab: "Why are they attacking?"
p5. Hiyab: "Oh, no..." | *Bzz | BZZ*
p6. Deleted | *Pop Pop Pop*
p7-8. Hiyab: "Come on, guys! It's town!"
p9-10. Hiyab: "Ok, now we can—" | *BOOM*

p1. *CRASH!!!* | Very, very, very, very small buildings
p2. Hiyab: "What the heck was that?!"
p3. Hiyab: "Where's the item baggy thingy?!"
p4. Fwed: "Um, Hiyab..."
p5. Hiyab: "What the lightningball is THAT?!" | *CRAKOW*
p6. Buddy: "It's like a whatchamacallit!"

p1. Hiyab: "A lightning ball."
p2. *BOOM*
p3. *BOOM*
p4. Hiyab/Buddy: "AAHHH!" | Fwed: "A banana!" | *Spit* | Banana: "HAHIHIHAHA!"

To Be Continued...

From Our Teen Authors

Ever-Learning yet Standing Tall

The Teen Author Workshop connects budding creatives with guidance on technique and genre. Facilitators help students from all backgrounds firm up their creativity through writing and art and their literacy skills for reading and writing. Students are challenged with writing prompts and peer feedback, tackling things from poems discussing the transition from youth to young adult or fantasy stories meant to capture an Audience. For our after school program, facilitators help students engage their creativity while spending time decompressing after school with fun activities. Students work solo and in groups throughout their time.

During publication preparation, students who submit pieces for the anthology have a chance to get their submissions reviewed by a professional editor who offers suggestions and notes for further growth as rising stars to help them prepare for outside publication in the future.

Briana Beel

I like to play soccer, basketball, and softball. I am good at drawing and music. I have one sibling and my family, and I live in Tennessee. I am in sixth grade, and in my free time I love to play video games, write stories, and play games outside. I have at least three businesses: making soap, making key chains, and creating books. When I grow up, I will be a nail tech and a hairstylist. I also have three goals I want to achieve: graduate college, become a nail tech professional, and own a house by the time I am 21.

THE MOVIE

Story Excerpt

One scary afternoon, I tell my mom I will be going to my friend's house. My mom says, "No, because it is 3:00 in the afternoon," But I say, "Mom, calm down, I am not *you*! This is my life, not yours!" Mom says, "Go, then, since you don't want to be me." She looks sad. When I leave, I start to feel bad, but I am right: this is my life. So, I am going to my friend's house.

I get this weird feeling, like somebody is following me. I look back, and I see a black car behind me; I try to go down the lane, but the person follows me. I tried to move away from that person, but he was so fast, and he had a gun in his hand. I could see Walmart, so I go there and he follows me in. I run away, and as I run faster, he runs even faster. I tried calling the police, but he caught me. I screamed; just then, he knocked me out with his gun. All I saw after was darkness.

To Be Continued...

Heidy Canales

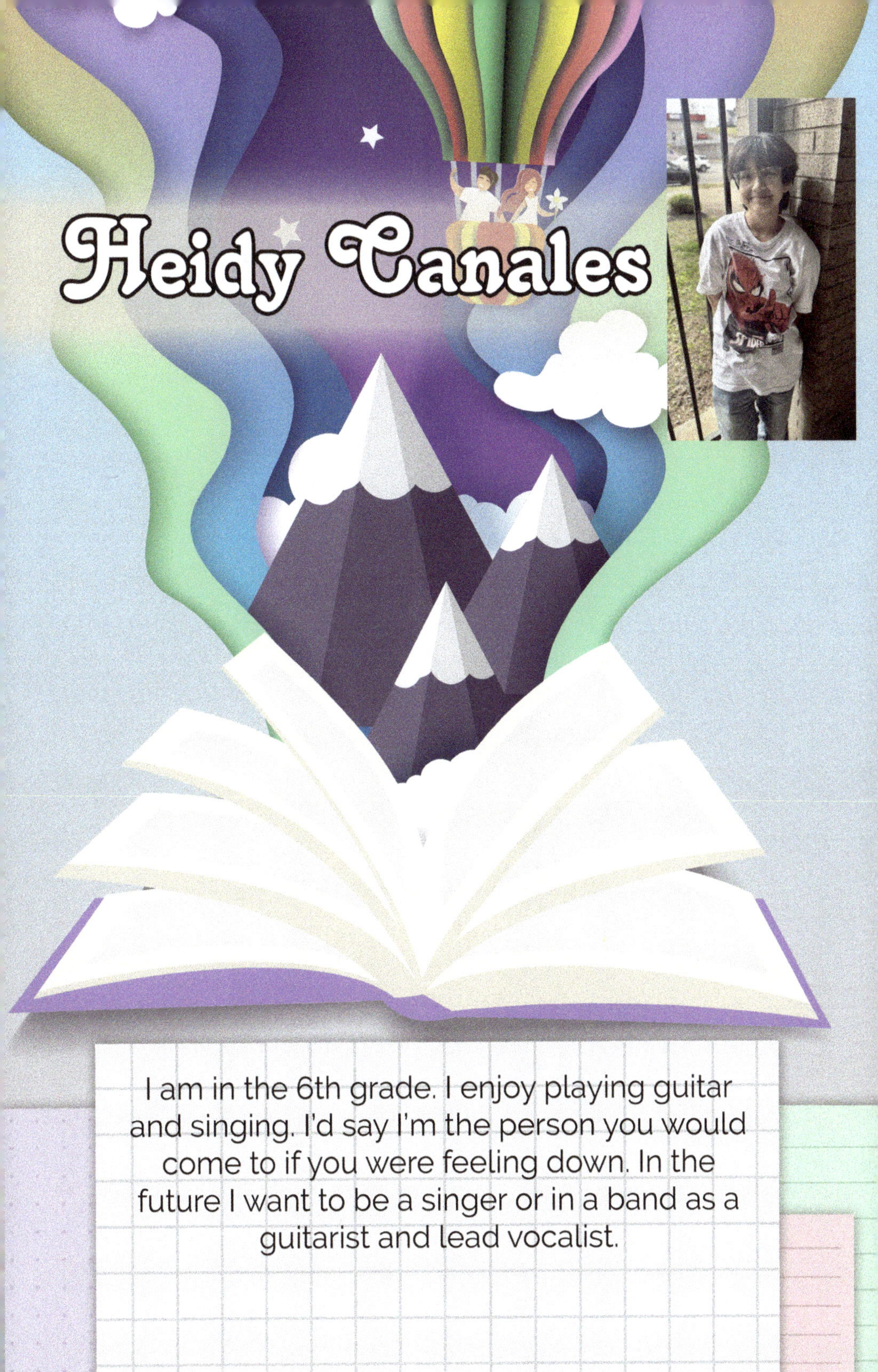

I am in the 6th grade. I enjoy playing guitar and singing. I'd say I'm the person you would come to if you were feeling down. In the future I want to be a singer or in a band as a guitarist and lead vocalist.

BLACKOUT POETRY

Art Project

Things I Like about Me

I love the texture of oil pastels
between my fingers,
the satisfaction of drawing
a perfect curve,
the cozy feeling
in drawing eye after eye.

I love the even back and forth
of swinging on my swing set
and the way it lets my mind fly.
I love how the oily smell of Pop's basement
makes my brain smile, how talking with Pop
about trains and myths
and how to build an engine from scratch
fills me with energy.

the familiar sound
of the *Lord of the Rings* soundtrack
every time Noelle and I
watch the movies together at her house,
and the calming sound
of Mr. Ames's voice
in the oasis of English class.

Sometimes I click my teeth
even though my dentist says I shouldn't
because my jaw likes to move
to the rhythm of songs
and chew on ice.

Sometimes I blink real hard
or squeeze my hands into fists
or scribble in my notebook
when the feelings inside me
are too big for words. I love the way
feelings pump through
my whole body like blood,

ow [alive] I am
om everything I feel.

ometimes I jump
ecause
ometimes you've just gotta jump.

ME VES?

Poem

Cuando te miro a los ojos, solo veo corazones.
La forma en que caminas, la forma en que hablas.
Cómo odio cómo yo te miro como un halcón.
Eres muy inteligente.
Es como si Dios te hubiera hecho como una obra de arte.
Ojalá pudieras verme como yo te veo a ti...

ME VES?
DO YOU SEE ME?

Poem, Translation

When I look you in the eyes, I only see hearts.
the way you walk, the way you talk.
How I hate how I look at you like a hawk.
You are very smart.
It is as if God made you like a work of art.
I wish you could see me as I see you...

Jonnyka Carter

I'm in the 6th grade. I joined the writing program because I like to write stories. I like to cheer, dance, play with my dog and cats, and hang out with my sister and friends, and I love to have family time or dinner dates with my family. I want to be a teacher or a cheer coach when I'm older.

Color-Changing Sky
Poem

The color-changing sky looks at me from up high
I look in a daze wondering why the sky looks so high
I look up, down, and around to see if I'm down to the ground
I looked up one last time to see the color-changing sky

Sisterly Concern
Short Story

One day, my friend and I had a bad fight about a rumor that wasn't true. I was sad and mad when I got home, so I plopped down on the couch. My sister saw me when she came in, but rather than ask a bunch of questions about what was wrong, she just sat next to me and waited until I had the words. She listened the whole time, letting me vent. Once I was done, she took me out for some ice cream and a nice walk through the park. She didn't bring the fight back up, and I started to feel a lot better.

Alyson Cordova

I used to love cartoons, but I forced myself to change and start liking anime just to fit in. After a while, I thought I had to change again to make others like me. But when I joined the writing program I'm in now, people appreciated me for who I am. They didn't judge me for what I like, and I finally felt accepted.

Not even Jan knows. But here I am with other people sharing my stories. Not feeling like a weirdo.

Thank you <3

A Different World

Poem

I like anime
'Cause it feels like home—
bright colors, big worlds,
stories that make me feel less alone.

Characters who fight,
characters who care,
they dream loud,
they feel deep,
and I see myself in there.

Some people don't get it,
and that's okay with me.
'Cause when I press play,
I'm exactly who I want to be.

Anime isn't just a show—
it's comfort, it's escape,
it's the place my heart goes
when it needs a little space.

So yeah, I like anime,
and I'm not afraid to say it.

Niños Extraviados

La ciudad era una bestia en expansión y sofocante, sus garras de hormigón cavando profundamente en el horizonte. Aquí, en el corazón de su caos, los ocho encontraron su santuario: el Distrito 9. No es un lugar en ningún mapa, sino una mentalidad, un territorio que habían reclamado con la noche, latidos implacables y letras garabateadas en cada superficie de su estudio.

Bang Chan, su ancla y arquitecto, pasó una mano por su cabello, con los ojos fijos en la demostración jugando a través de sus auriculares. A su lado, Changbin era un torbellino de intensidad enfocada, garabateando líneas en su cuaderno con un bolígrafo que se movía tan rápido como su rap de fuego rápido. Han, encaramado en una silla giratoria, rebotó su pierna al ritmo, una sonrisa traviesa en su rostro mientras improvisaba una nueva melodía vocal. Los tres, miembros de 3RACHA, fueron una tormenta de energía creativa, un testimonio constante de su arte autoproducido y sin remordimientos.

Pero esta noche, la energía se sintió diferente. Una tensión tranquila colgaba en el aire. Al coro final de su nueva canción le faltaba algo. Estaba destinado a ser explosivo, un rugido desafiante contra el ruido, pero se sentía... plano.

"¿Y si nos estamos esforzando demasiado?" Han preguntó, empujando su cabello hacia atrás en frustración. "Parece que estamos cocinando, pero el plato falta el ingrediente secreto."

Chan finalmente se quitó los auriculares, pasando una mano por su cara cansada. "Tal vez tienes razón. Tomemos un descanso. Todos para un soplo de aire fresco."

Se derramaron fuera del estudio y en la fuga de incendios, donde las luces de la ciudad se extendían debajo de ellos como una constelación brillante. La lluvia se había detenido, y el aire estaba limpio y frío. El sonido familiar del ruido de la ciudad, la energía constante y pulsante, ahora se sentía diferente.

"Es como nuestro propio mundo aquí," dijo Félix, su voz profunda llevando el viento.

"Sí," estuvo de acuerdo Hyunjin, apoyado en la barandilla. "Todo el ruido, el caos... todo sigue ahí, pero es nuestro. Lo controlamos."

De repente, los ojos de Han se iluminaron. Volvió al estudio, una energía salvaje que volvía a sus movimientos. "¡Eso es todo!" Exclamó. "¡El ruido! ¡Necesitamos hacer que el ruido sea parte de la música!"

En unos momentos, los ocho estaban de vuelta dentro, el agotamiento reemplazado por una oleada de fervor creativo. Chan sacó la pista, y con un nuevo propósito, comenzaron a ponerse en capas en sonidos - una línea de bajo distorsionada que imitaba el estruendo de la ciudad, un sintetizador agudo y penetrante que se sentía como un relámpago. Cuando la música llegó a su punto más alto esta vez, ya no era solo una canción. Era un himno. Era un sonido crudo y sin filtrar que encapsulaba el hermoso caos de la ciudad, sus propias luchas y la fuerza que encontraron para enfrentarlo todo juntos.

Una ola colectiva de alivio los arrasó, explotando en una ráfaga de vítores y altos cinco. Era más que una canción; era un símbolo de su lucha continua para crear su propio camino.

"No solo es bueno," dijo Hyunjin, una sonrisa genuina en su rostro. "Es honesto. Es real."

"Todos nosotros," agregó I. N., su voz principal firme y segura.

Esa noche, dejaron el estudio no como ocho individuos sino como un grupo. El laberinto de la ciudad ya no era una amenaza, sino una parte de su propio sonido. Ellos eran los que habían "traído" de la norma, tallando su propio camino en un mundo que trataba de contenerlos. Y con cada latido, cada letra, se aseguraron de que sus huellas fueran

Niños Extraviados: Stray Kids

Short Story - Translation

The city was a suffocating, ever-expanding beast, its concrete claws digging deep into the horizon. Here, in the heart of its chaos, the eight of them found their sanctuary: District 9. Not a place on any map, but a mindset—a territory they had claimed with the night, relentless heartbeats, and lyrics scribbled across every surface of their studio.

Bang Chan, their anchor and architect, ran a hand through his hair, eyes fixed on the demo playing through his headphones. Beside him, Changbin was a whirlwind of focused intensity, scribbling lines into his notebook with a pen that moved as fast as his rapid-fire rap. Han, perched on a spinning chair, bounced his leg to the rhythm, a mischievous smile on his face as he improvised a new vocal melody. The three of them—members of 3RACHA—were a storm of creative energy, a constant testament to their unapologetic, self-produced artistry.

But tonight, the energy felt different. A quiet tension hung in the air. The final chorus of their new song was missing something. It was meant to be explosive, a defiant roar against the noise, but it felt... flat.

"What if we're trying too hard?" Han asked, pushing his hair back in frustration. "It's like we're cooking, but the dish is missing that secret ingredient."

Chan finally pulled off his headphones, running a tired hand over his face. "Maybe you're right. Let's take a break. Everyone—fresh air."

The band spilled out of the studio onto the fire escape, where the city lights stretched below them like a glowing constellation. The rain had stopped, and the air was clean and cool.

The familiar sound of the city—its constant, pulsing energy—felt different now.

"It's like our own world up here," Felix said, his deep voice carried by the wind.

"Yeah," Hyunjin agreed, leaning against the railing. "All the noise, the chaos… it's still there, but it's ours. We control it."

Suddenly, Han's eyes lit up. He rushed back into the studio, a wild energy returning to his movements.

"That's it!" he exclaimed. "The noise! We need to make the noise part of the music!"

Within moments, all eight of them were back inside, exhaustion replaced by a surge of creative fire. Chan pulled up the track, and with a renewed sense of purpose, they began layering sounds—a distorted bass line that echoed the rumble of the city, a sharp, piercing synth that struck like lightning. When the music reached its peak this time, it was no longer just a song.

It was an anthem.

It was a raw, unfiltered sound that captured the city's beautiful chaos, their own struggles, and the strength they found in facing it all together.

A wave of relief washed over them, bursting into cheers and high-fives. It was more than a song; it was a symbol of their ongoing fight to carve their own path.

"It's not just good," Hyunjin said, a genuine smile on his face. "It's honest. It's real."

"All of us," I.N. added, his voice steady and sure.

That night, they left the studio not as eight individuals, but as one group. The maze of the city was no longer a threat—it had become part of their sound. They were the ones who broke away from the norm, carving their own path in a world that tried to confine them.

And with every beat, every lyric, they made sure their footprints would last.

The Girl Who Painted the Sky

Short Story

The town of Halewick was small enough that everyone knew when someone new arrived — yet that morning, the sky itself seemed to announce it.

A sudden spill of orange light broke through weeks of gray, and the townspeople said it felt like the weather was breathing again.

Amara was the new girl— quiet, hair always smudged with paint, living in the cottage at the edge of the lake. She came every morning to the water's edge, setting up her easel to paint the sunrise no one else bothered to look at anymore.

Eli worked at the lighthouse. He wasn't the kind who believed in signs or stories, just in routine: turning gears, checking lamps, keeping things steady. But one morning, he saw her— this girl painting like she was trying to fix the world —and something inside him shifted.

He started leaving the light on a few minutes longer, even after sunrise, just to see her reflection in the water. She noticed, of course, and one day she walked up the hill to the lighthouse with two cups of coffee and said:

> "You're the reason my mornings last longer."

They spent weeks talking about everything and nothing. She told him she painted skies because they changed faster than hearts. He told her he didn't believe that.

But one night, a storm rolled in— the kind that made the sea roar and the sky tear itself apart. Her cottage flooded, her paintings washed away, and Eli found her standing knee-deep in water, watching the colors swirl into the lake.

He pulled her close and said, "You can paint the sky again tomorrow."

She whispered, "Only if you promise to watch it with me."

When the storm cleared, they rebuilt her easel together.

And that morning, the sunrise didn't just belong to her.

It belonged to both of them— two people who taught each other that love, like the sky, doesn't need to be perfect to be beautiful.

A Different Place

Poem

My week's been fine.
Not as fine
For example, I feel away from here.

Some may ask "why do you look sad?"
Friends say "I'm okay,"
But in reality, I feel away

It's hard to be a good-grade kid.
But who cares, I can do anything. Right?
Friends say I'm a weirdo, talking too much.
That's how I show I'm comfortable with you.

You say to go away.
But do I have too?

When you realize it, it's too late.
You say to come back.
Now I won't be back.
I'm away forever till I feel fine.

But now it's getting to me.
I walk a different path. Away from you.
Someone who wants me not you.
I might sound selfish. But I'm not.

Forgotten Kid

It was my birthday.
My mom got pizza for my class
I felt happy... well, not really

"It's your day to be happy."
Every year, I sometimes feel happy
I feel like I'm in someone else's body, celebrating someone
else's birthday. I'm happy home like a puppy getting a treat.

My mom gets the cake out.
As I'm about to blow out the candles, my baby brother, he
wants to blow out the candles.
He does blow out the candles.
Forgotten.... Forgotten.... Forgotten, that's the word.
I felt forgotten.

That night I looked out the window. It's raining.
My eyes are glossy and glass like the rain.
My mom came in asking why I'm crying
I just felt forgotten.

Savannah Dunigan

I enjoy doing hair, dancing, singing, and watching horror. I am good at braiding hair. I would describe myself as a funny, nerdy, and anime-obsessed person. In the future, I want to be a hairstylist.

How do you love yourself in the dark?
Poem

She always asked if she was okay, telling people she needs help in her own way. Scared what people will say, looking in the mirror, scared to break the glass when she's a person who can't recognize herself. She hides in the dark, making sure she doesn't leave her mark in the world, her heart turned cold, she tries as she grows. She wants to love or see the world above all the hatred and sadness and only wants happiness.

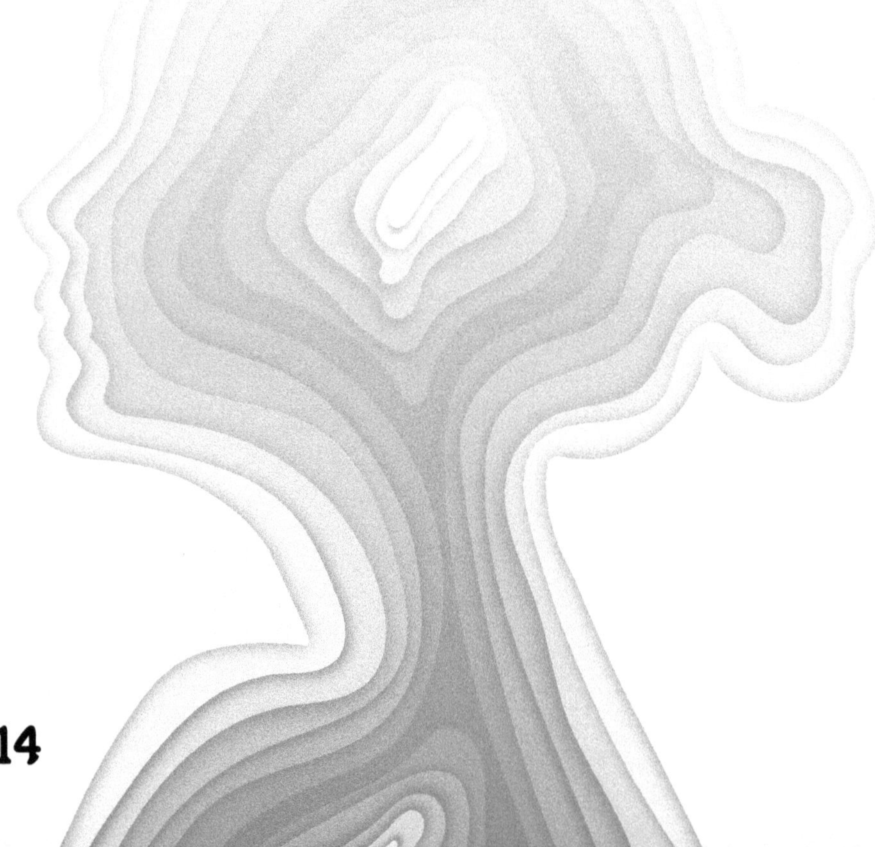

Asael Garcia

I was born in Tennessee. Some of my hobbies are sports and traveling. My favorite foods are pasta, pizza, and tamales. When I grow up, I want to live somewhere different. I joined Carnegie Writers to help me write more and read.

Surviving the Crash

In 2018, I was driving home when I suddenly lost control of the steering wheel and hit a sign that made the car flip and roll down the forest I had been driving beside. When I started to roll, I hit the window of the car and passed out.

When I woke up, I heard my ears ringing, and I couldn't move my body. I realized that I had rolled down the forest miles away, and there wouldn't be anyone that would hear me. I spent about two hours trying to get out of the crushed car, and when I did, I passed out. When I woke up, I started to look for wood to make fire, so I could stay warm in the night. I remembered that I had a lighter in the back of the trunk. When I opened the crushed car lid trunk, I found the lighter and lit the wood on fire.

The next day I woke up and thought about what I could do so people could see where I was. I got the idea to light the crushed car on fire, so people could see the smoke and call for rescuers. I waited about three hours until rescuers came and found me. They took me to the hospital and asked me what had happened. I told them everything and after that I passed out.

STRANDED ISLAND
Short Story

In 2003, I, Alexander, was preparing for another regular flight for the military air force to scout out an island. I noticed the fuel of the jet was lower than usual, but I didn't think much of it because it had happened before, and the fuel didn't run out. I was 3-4 hours into scouting the island when the jet started to warn me about fuel running out. I tried sending warnings to the air force, but they didn't respond. The jet started to crash down, so I directed the jet into the water. When the plane impacted on the water, I felt my head hit the window and break the glass. Luckily, I had a life jacket, so I was able to get out of the jet.

I knew the longest I would stay on the island would be about 1-3 days, because as soon as the day ended the air force would notice I was missing and send a rescue team to come and look for me. When I got to the island, I started looking for rocks, wood, and sticks to make a fire and stay warm. I then climbed a palm tree to rip out some leaves to use them as coverage. When the night came, the wind made waves hit the shore and soak me wet. I started to feel really cold, to the point I couldn't sleep.

Around 3 in the morning, I heard a helicopter passing by and saw flashing lights. I knew it had to be the rescue team, so I lit a stick on fire and threw it in the air. They were able to find me because of it and take me into the helicopter. When they got me into the helicopter, I passed out. When I woke up, I was being checked by doctors to see if I had any injuries or diseases. After a week, the hospital let me go back to work, and the military gave me a 10k check for what had happened.

CONTRACT FOR A LIFE

Story Excerpt

In 2024, a person named Robert the Fourth attended a meeting for a top agency about a life-changing invention. The agency had told him if he wanted to be a part of the invention, he had to sign a contract, which would not allow him to tell anyone about what he saw and heard in the meeting. Robert did not have any choice because he was going broke; the other project he worked on for five years had failed badly.

After Robert had signed the contract, they took him into a dark room where he saw a large machine that had a glass door, which looked like it could fit two people inside. Then three scientists came into the room and explained that they had made a machine capable of time travel. When Robert heard that, he did not believe them and was about to walk away when a scientist told him to hold on and try it for himself if he didn't believe them. Robert stepped into the machine thinking nothing would happen when a screen lit up with past and future years popping up on it. Suddenly, the machine started flashing white lights and Robert passed out.

When Robert woke up, he wasn't in the room anymore, but in a jungle. Robert started to wander into the jungle, making noises as he walked, when he suddenly saw a huge python that was wrapped

119

up in a tree. Robert's natural instincts kicked in, and he started to run back to the time machine. When he got into the time machine, he clicked the button that said 'back' and left.

To Be Continued...

La Noche

Poem

El cielo se oscurece,
el sol se duerme,
la luna despierta,
y las estrellas empiezan a brillar,
porque la noche a empezado

La Noche: Night

Poem Translation

The sky starts to darken
The sun goes to sleep
The moon awakens
And the stars start to shine
Because the night has begun

Cameron Hudson

I am Cameron, and I am in 8th grade. I play PS5, Xbox, and Nintendo Switch and watch videos. I am good at soccer. I want to be a firefighter. I speak English and have eight siblings.

Writing a Fairytale
Short Story

Once upon a time, I was in fairytale land.

In my fairytale, I lived in a castle with the king, queen, and knights. The queen asked for a cup of tea and wore a tiara, while the king wore a crown. They sat happily on their thrones and protected the castle from dragons. But then we felt sorry for the dragon, so I included him in our family. Everyone was happy and had strawberry cake together.

The Rainbow Vine

Once upon a time, a girl named Rhonda in fairytale land noticed that the rainbow vine's leaves were drying out. The king and queen of fairytale land, alongside the seven dwarves, wanted to save the rainbow vine, so Rhonda went on an adventure to get sparkling water.

A witch suddenly arrives and tries to stop Rhonda from getting the sparkling water for the rainbow vine. Luckily, Rhonda has her own powers, so she stops the witch. With the which gone, Rhonda reaches the sparkling lake and retrieves the water needed to save the rainbow vine. Everyone was happy because with the vine saved, fairytale land's magic would last forever.

GOING

I love going camping with my family
I like going on hikes in the woods
I like going around the world, around the USA,
going to lakes and cities, going on ships

Braelyn Jones

I'm in the 7th grade. I love cheering, dancing, singing, and playing instruments. People say I'm good with constructive criticism and good at different types of art. When I'm older, I hope I will be professional at dance, cheer, singing, and acting. Cool things about me are that I keep trying, learn really fast, have a great personality, and I also am learning multiple languages.

Game or Reality
Playwriting

Characters:

Priyah, early 30s, Leah's older sister
Emma, 7, Priyah's daughter
Lisa, 14, Priyah's daughter
Leah, early 30s, Priyah's younger sister
Lilly, 7, Leah's daughter
Maya, 13, Leah's daughter

[**Scene 1**]

[Setting: PRIYAH's Living Room]

EMMA
I miss Lisa; she should have been here by
now.

MAYA
Don't worry, she will be here soon.

LISA walks in the door and yells down the hall.

LISA
I'm home!

EMMA
Lissaa! I really missed you!

EMMA runs up and hugs LISA, who smiles and
returns the hug.

LISA
I missed you too, Emma!

LILLY storms into the room.

LILLY
Come on, let's go upstairs and play our
new video game.

LILLY runs out of the room.

EMMA, LISA, and MAYA all reply "Ok!" together,
pushing and shoving each other as they raced up
the stairs.

[**Scene 2**]

[Setting: PRIYAH's Living Room]

PRIYAH [hollering]
Kids, time for dinner!

LILLY
Hey Maya, I bet can get to the dinner
table before you.

MAYA
Bet!

EMMA
1…2…3…Go!

[**Scene 3**]

[Setting: EMMA's Room]

PRIYAH [off-stage]
If you are finished you can go play on

your video game for an hour before bed.

MAYA [off-stage]
Let's go!

All four cousins run up the stairs.

MAYA
Let's play 'House fire nightmare.'

LISA
I don't know, that seems so real.

MAYA
It will be fine.

EMMA
I am scared.

LISA
It's ok, Emma.

The girls put on VR headsets and turn the game on.

MAYA
Where are y'all at?

LISA
Me and Emma are at house 103.

LILLY
I'm at house 100.

MAYA
Ok, Lilly. I will meet you at 100

The girls spend around 20 minutes playing the game.

EMMA
Do you guys' smell smoke?

EMMA takes off the headset, looking around the room. LISA rips hers off.

LISA [screaming]
The house is on fire!

LILLY [scared]
What do we do?

LISA
Stay calm, we have to find Mom and Aunt Leah.

PRIYAH & LEAH [off-stage]
Girls!

All the girls rush down the stairs.

[Scene 4]

[Setting: PRIYAH's living room]

All four cousins storm down the stairs, yelling for their mothers.

EMMA
Do you smell that?

LISA
The house is on fire!

PRIYAH [scolding]
It is not! That is not funny girls.

LISA, LILLY, EMMA, and MAYA all look to each other,

confused, before turning and walking silently back upstairs. They can still smell something burning.

[End Scene]

I am and in the 6th grade. My favorite hobbies are writing poems and being active. My talents are writing poems, singing, and enjoying sports. My personality is investigative. I would like to become a lawyer. Something unique about me is that I can describe emotions well.

LOST IN LANGUAGE

Why do I fall, God,
and feel like I can't get up?
Why do I try so hard
yet still end up on my knees,
hands shaking,
heart trembling,
wondering if You still see me
in the dark?

I whisper Your name,
but sometimes the silence answers louder.
And I ask,
"Lord, why does the ground know me better
than the sky ever has?"
Why do the storms come
one after another,
wave after wave,
until I forget what calm feels like?

Why do I fall, God,
when all I want is to stand?
I thought faith meant strength,
but sometimes faith feels like
holding onto a rope
that's fraying in my hands.
I slip,
I stumble,

I break,
and I wonder if You still reach for me.

Maybe You do.
Maybe the falling
isn't punishment
but the place where You meet me.
Maybe the ground
is where Your mercy gathers,
where Your grace sits and waits
for me to breathe again.

But still I ask—
Why me?
Why this?
Why now?

Why does my heart feel heavy
like it carries storms
too big for its own size?
Why does life knock me down
right when I'm learning to walk?
Why do I cry in secret
and smile in public,
as if the world expects strength
from a soul that's crumbling?

Why do I fall, God,
and feel like You're far?
Even though You promised
never to leave,
never to forsake.

I know that promise,
I repeat it,
I hold it like a lifeline—
but some nights the darkness
speaks louder than truth.

Still...
somewhere in the breaking,
somewhere in the bruised places,
I feel a whisper not from the world
but from You:

"Child, the ground you fall on
is not the end—
it's the beginning.
I lift those who cannot lift themselves.
I carry those who have no strength left.
I build warriors
from the pieces of the broken."

So maybe I fall
not because I'm weak,
but because You're teaching me
how to rise with Your strength
and not my own.

Maybe I can't get up
because You're waiting
for me to finally say,
"Lord, I need You."
Maybe the rising
starts the moment

I stop pretending
I can do it alone.

But God...
if I'm honest,
I'm tired.
My spirit aches.
My heart feels thin
like paper in the rain.
So I come to You
bruised, weary, trembling—
and I lay all of it
at Your feet.

If falling is part of my journey,
then let Your hands be the place I land.
If rising is still ahead,
then give me the strength
my soul cannot find on its own.

Because even if I fall a thousand times,
I believe—
even shakily—
that You will lift me a thousand and one.

So here I am, God,
not strong,
not perfect,
but reaching.

Pick me up
when I can't get up myself.

Hold me
when my heart breaks slow.
Guide me
when I lose my way in the dark.

And remind me
every time I fall
that I'm still Yours,
still seen,
still loved,
and never too far gone
for You to lift me again.

Destiny to Heal

Poem

Why can't people heal?
Maybe because healing is not a straight line,
not a road with signs
or a map that tells you, "You're almost there."
Sometimes it's a broken path
where every step reminds you
of the moment you first learned how to hurt.

Some hearts don't heal
because they were taught to hide their pain,
told to keep silent,
to swallow the storm until it drowned their voice.
Some were told to "stay strong,"
not realizing strength sometimes means
falling apart long enough
to put yourself back together.

Some people can't heal
because the ones who hurt them
never apologized,
never cared,
never looked back.
And the emptiness left behind
keeps whispering lies like,
"You deserved it,"
even though that was never true.

Some can't heal
because memories live inside their bones—
heavy like stones in a river,
refusing to wash away
no matter how hard the water runs.
Some wounds stay open
because the mind keeps replaying moments
it desperately wishes it could rewrite.

Some people can't heal
because life didn't give them time.
Pain stacked on pain,
loss layered on loss,
like storms piling over oceans
with no calm in between.
And when you're always fighting to stay afloat,
you never get the breath you need to mend.

Some can't heal
because healing means facing the truth—
the truth that someone they loved broke them,
that someone they trusted left them,
that someone they needed
walked away without looking back.
Sometimes healing means grieving
what should have been,
not just what was.

Some people can't heal
because they heal others instead.
They're the ones who give light

but sit in the dark,
who lift everyone else
while sinking quietly
under the weight of their own heart.
They pour and pour
until there's nothing left
but the ache of being empty.

And some can't heal
because they don't believe they deserve it.
Pain can lie like that—
make you think you're unworthy of peace,
unworthy of joy,
unworthy of being whole again.
But you are.
You always were.

Maybe people can't heal
because healing isn't simple,
isn't quick,
isn't perfect.
It's messy,
it's slow,
it's breaking and rebuilding
again and again
until one day the pieces fit
in a new way you never expected.

But here's the truth:
People can heal.
They heal in moments,

in breaths,
in quiet victories no one sees.
They heal when they choose to stay,
when they choose to try,
when they choose to believe
there's still something worth fighting for
inside their tired, tender heart.

Healing is not a finish line—
it's a journey back to yourself.
And even if it takes years,
even if you stumble a thousand times,
your heart is still learning,
still growing,
still rising from the ashes
it once thought would bury it.

So maybe the question isn't,
"Why can't people heal?"
but
"How brave are they for trying every day?"

And the answer is:
braver than they know.

Rude Awakening

Why do they ask me
to stand so straight,
to smile so clean,
to hold my chin high
even when the weight of the world
presses my shoulders to the floor?

Why am I expected
to be the perfect picture—
uncracked, untouched, unshaken—
when inside I'm trembling,
when my spirit is bent,
when I'm one breath away
from breaking in half?

They look at me like I'm a painting
hanging on a spotless wall,
like my colors can't run,
like my frame can't splinter,
like I'm meant to be admired,
not understood.
But they don't see the storms
that rage underneath the brush strokes,
the battle scars hidden beneath
the pretty little edges.

Why do I have to be strong

when strength is the one thing
I ran out of?
Why do I have to hold it together
when it's my heart that's falling apart
piece by piece—
quiet enough that no one hears it,
loud enough that I feel it echo
all night long?

People love the version of me
that shines,
the version that laughs at pain
and makes it look easy—
the one who rises from ashes
like it's just another morning routine.
But they never ask
how much the fire burned me
before I stood back up.

Why do I have to be perfect
when I fall?
Why must every mistake
be softened,
every tear be hidden,
every crack be painted over
so the world won't see
that I'm human
and hurting
and healing in slow, uneven ways?

Maybe they don't understand
that even angels stumble,

that even the strongest hearts
have nights where they crumble,
that even the brightest souls
carry shadows.

I'm tired of being a masterpiece
when I'm meant to be a person.
I'm tired of pretending
that falling doesn't bruise me,
that breaking doesn't scare me,
that I don't bleed,
that I don't ache,
that I don't sometimes want someone
to just say,
"It's okay to not be okay."

Why do I have to be the perfect picture
when I fall?
I shouldn't.
I don't.
I won't.

Because there is beauty
in the broken places,
in the way I rise slowly,
in the way I piece myself back together
with trembling hands
and stubborn hope.

Because the real masterpiece
isn't the picture they want—
the flawless, untouched, shining you.

The real masterpiece
is the truth:
you survived the fall,
you stood back up,
and you kept going
even when everything in you
wanted to stay down.

That is the kind of perfect
no picture can capture—
but every soul
can feel.

Joy Nuñez

I'm currently writing a book (that might be the one you're reading!). Let's get to know me: my hobbies are drawing, reading, and watching anime, (I've only started three, but it's progress, okay?). I started drawing in 2nd grade, and I've been improving ever since! I love it, and one day I want to be an artist and a fashion designer. I'm currently in 6th grade. According to my wonderful friends, I'm a little weird, funny, and jolly in the best way possible.

The Last Entry

"It's been seven years since I found this book," Karla mused to her best friend Miley. "And you've seen how it seems to write down everything I've been through." She held up the book, careful not to smudge her freshly painted nails. "I still can't help but wonder…"

"Why you?" Miley finished, staring at the book. The pair had been friends since they were born, so she often knew what Karla was thinking. "To be honest, me too."

As the besties pondered the book, it seemed to shift in Karla's hands. Miley perked up, wondering what it had written. For some reason, it seemed different to her, like something was weighing it down.

Karla noticed Miley's eagerness towards the book, and she asked, "Miley what did you see?"

"Oh, it's just the book seemed to write something new!" Miley squealed. "Nothing has happened to you today yet, so maybe it's telling your future, or maybe even your soulmate!"

"It can't be, it doesn't predict my future; it only writes what I've—" While she was talking, the book opened in her hand and started writing. Karla stared at the words, a chill running down her spine. "…what…" She turned the book over so Miley could see what was written. First confusion, then horror spread across her face.

"K-karla," Miley managed, tears forming in her eyes before falling down her cheeks. "I thought it only writes what you've been through…right?" Her voice cracked with each word. The silence stretched between them, Karla lost in her own thoughts.

Why…why me? Will I actually die?!

Miley started pacing as she sobbed, "Oh my God, oh my God, oh my God, oh my God!" She stopped abruptly, wailing, "I don't want you to die, Karlita!" She plopped down on the floor wailing, sobbing, even begging Pandora, Karla's fourteen-year-old cat, to somehow stop this nightmare. Karla was standing there, still zoned out, but Miley's wails startled her. She moved to sit on the floor by her friend, pulling her into a hug.

"*Miley*! I promise everything's going to be okay!" Miley sniffled and curled up in Karla's little safe haven, her hugs. "And why were you begging to sweet old Pandora?" Karla asked in a playful tone, staring down at Miley, whose expression broke into a grin. They both started laughing, but they knew: laughing wasn't going to solve this mystery.

***

The next day, Karla was driving to school while Miley sang her heart out to "Hit Me Baby (One More Time)" by Britney Spears. Both girls were trying to ignore thinking about what happened yesterday with the book.

"Miley, you are making my *ears bleed*!" Karla said, covering her ears; as soon as she let go of the wheel, the car swerved. Miley screamed, and Karla quickly grabbed the wheel again.

"Eyes on the road, Karla!" Miley yelled at her. "Not even your eyes, *hands on the wheel*!!"

"It was your screeching's fault!" Karla yelled back.

Offended, Miley scoffed: "*First of all*, that was singing; second of all, I sing great, excuse you!"

Karla sighed. "I'm sorry… let's just forget this. We are here, anyways."

Miley looked away, pouting, but they got out of the car and entered their school, where both girls were currently tenth grade sophomores. Life inside Lincoln High went on as usual: the jocks were trying to impress girls, the theater kids were doing theater kid stuff, the CCP (Cute Cool Popular) girls were gossiping and obsessing over guys, the "outcasts" were doing weird kid stuff, and finally, the normal people were doing normal things. Miley and Karla weren't in any of these groups; they were known as "the best duo of all time", which Karla found stupid.

"Ughhh, I hate first period!" Miley whined.

"It's not that bad, right?"

"Easy for you to say. You're a good student. The teachers are nice to you."

Karla snorted. "The teachers expect a lot of me, you mean..." As they entered their classroom, they noticed Mr. Peterson writing on the whiteboard: Pop Quiz Today! Karla looked at Miley. "I see your point about first period."

Mr. Peterson was grinning ear to ear, which usually happens on a pop quiz day. He loved ruining the high schoolers' day. The girls moved to sit beside each other, each in a desk. Eventually, the class settled down, and Mr. Peterson handed each student their quiz, one by one. "Everyone, you will have thirty minutes to finish this test," he announced gleefully. "You may now begin!" They all started; Karla blew through quickly, but Miley got stuck on the first question. After the thirty minutes, Mr. Peterson grabbed the tests, again one by one.

Miley leaned over to whisper to Karla: "I'm screwed!"

"You'll be fine! Trust me."

"No, I won't!"

Karla sighed and looked out the window. Her eyes widened: a car was speeding right for her window. Karla jumped up and bolted across the classroom, yelling to get the other students away as well. As the sound of shattering glass and crunched metal joined the screams, some of the kids tripped and others covered themselves from debris. Desks were upended or sent flying, and papers scattered everywhere.

Around them, the dust and debris settled into a strained silence. When Karla carefully looked up, she saw that no one was driving the car. No one.

To Be Continued...

Porque Yo?

Short Story

Un día, me desperté de mi cama, por supuesto era un día normal, como siempre. Me cepillé los dientes y luego bajé las escaleras. Para mi sorpresa, había mucha gente vestida de negro y llorando como si alguien murió. Cuando fui a preguntar que estaban haciendo, alguien pasó por mi, como si fuera un fantasma. Obviamente, me di la vuelta y le dije, gritando, "OYE, ¿ino puedes ver que estoy parada aquí!?" Pero nada, nada pasó, no me dijo nada. Me di cuenta de algo, algo muy muy horrible, yo era la persona muerta, yo era la persona que perdieron.

Porque Yo? Why Me?

Short Story Translation

One day, I woke up from my bed, of course it was a normal day, as always. I brushed my teeth and then went downstairs. To my surprise, there were many people dressed in black and crying as if someone died. When I went to ask what they were doing, someone passed by me, as if I were a ghost. Obviously, I turned around and said, yelling, "Hey! Can't you see I'm standing here!?" But nothing... nothing happened, he didn't say anything to me. I realized something, something very, very horrible, I was the dead person, I was the person they lost.

BLACKOUT POETRY
Art Project

Emanuel Pimental-Aguirre

I'm in the sixth grade. I like to do karate, and I like to eat lot of food, and I'm double jointed My favorite food is tacos, and my favorite color is black. I like social studies and science. I'm good at soccer and video games too. How I describe myself is I'm funny, nice, cool, and sometimes I can be mean. My goal is to earn a black belt in the future. A fun fact is I'm the only boy in the family. One important thing to me is my personality.

Yellow

Bob had a problem. No one liked him because he was yellow, so he was lonely and sad. One day at Banff National Park, he met another yellow boy named Manny. Manny had moved to Alberta, Canada from Nashville, Tennessee. They became best friends and tried to find others with yellow skin. However, they couldn't find anyone.

One day, Manny caught a serious illness and passed away. When Manny died, no one but Bob and Manny's family came to the funeral. Bob was devastated and became determined to find a cure for his yellow skin.

Eventually he succeeded, celebrating the cure, but he was still sad because he was alone.

THE TORNADO

Short Story

On a dark and stormy day, my sister Isabel, my cousin Victoria, and I were playing a game named *Dead Rail* when Isabel said, "Guys, there is a tornado warning over here." She looked scared, and Victoria and I got scared too. I ran to tell my mom, but she was asleep. I woke her up and told her there was tornado warning. She said, "It's ok, we will be fine," in a calm voice with a soothing expression, but we heard the tornado siren. Then my sister said she saw the tornado forming, so my aunt grabbed Xander, William, and Emilia while my mom grabbed the pets. My aunt told all of us kids to lay down in the bathroom while my eldest sister Mimi started praying. Later, my aunt told us the tornado almost hit the ground nearby, but we survived.

Ian Michael Robinson

...I like reading graphic novels and watching anime like *Toilet-bound Hanako-kun* and *SpyxFamily*. I also like cooking with my dad; we do things like baking and cooking dinner. I would love to live in Japan. Carnegie Writer taught me how to write a story, which I wanted to learn how to do. Now, I am being put in a book.

The Person on the Other Side

Short Story

"What's your name?" the person on the other side of the phone asked.

"Jisoo," I answered.

"Jisoo?"

"Yes!" I replied.

"Where are you?" the person asked.

"Home."

"Oh... Me too!"

"Ahhh," I replied, confused.

"Where do you live?" they asked next.

"Hotel."

"Me, too."

"...cool..." I wasn't sure what to say.

"What room are you in?" the phone person asked.

"101," I responded hesitantly.

"Me, too!" The phone person stated.

I didn't say anything. How could they live in the

same room? I was alone.

"Hello?" they called.

"Yes?" I answered against my better judgment.

"Are you… alone?"

I paused before answering, "Yes…why?" Some of my fear slipped into my voice.

"No reason," the voice whispered.

I heard noises in my room. "Wait…" I heard the noise again. What could that be? It sounded like someone moving around. "I think someone's in my room; I am going to check it out."

"Why?" The person asked.

I ignored the question, simply calling out to the room, "Hello?" No one answered. I heard the phone click as the call ended, and quickly tried to call back. A voice comes on, stating robotically, "the number you called has been disconnected." I looked at the phone, puzzled. I could hear something behind me.

YOU KNOW?

Story Excerpt

May 17th, 1980

Hello, it's me Aiko, and welcome to my new notebook for journaling about my summer.

May 18th, 1980

Hello, it's me Aiko again. Today, my friends asked me to come to a party with them, but my mom said, "Don't even think about it, Aiko Lola Lee!" So I will just sneak out.

May 19th, 1980

Hello, it's me Aiko again. Last night I had so much fun! I met this cute boy named Teo, and I got his number.

May 23rd, 1980

Hello, it's me. Aiko. Again. I know I haven't been writing in a lot. But something's… off… about Teo. He calls me at all hours of the night, sometimes 2 in the morning, asking me to go places, but he never shows up.

May 24th, 1980

I had a weird phone call with Teo today. I asked him what he was up to, and he said nothing much. Before we could talk about anything else, he started sounding awkward and said he had to go but asked if I would meet for lunch. I hesitated, but said ok. Hopefully he's there this time.

* * *

"In tonight's news... Young Aiko Lola Lee has now been missing for three days. If you have seen this young woman, please contact the police."

* * *

"It has now been one full week since Aiko Lola Lee vanished. Her parents are desperate for any information. If you know anything about her disappearance, please contact the police."

To Be Continued...

The Curse of the Warped Records

Story Excerpt

While investigating the death of a local doctor, introverted actor Akihiko Lee uncovered a legend about a supernaturally cursed warped record circulating throughout Korea. As soon as anyone uses the record, that person has exactly 124 days left to live. The doomed few appear like ordinary people; however, they are invisible in photographs and icy to the touch, almost like the stories about vampires. Aiko found this record and went to grab it, refusing to believe in the superstition. As he picks it up, a collage of images flashes into his mind: a violent fox balancing on a wide doctor, an old newspaper headline with a pointless story, a hooded bear ranting about eyes, and a drinking well located in a sleepy place.

When Akihiko came to, he noticed his hands turning wolf; he realized the curse of the warped record is true and called on his best friend, Finn Smith, a singer, actor, songwriter, to help with the curse. Finn examined the record and willingly submitted himself to the curse. The same visions flashed before his eyes, and he found the violent fox balancing on a wide doctor particularly chilling. He joined the queue for a supernatural death.

Aiko and Finn pursue a quest to uncover the meaning of the visions, starting with a search for the hooded bear. Yet the biggest question will be if they can solve the curse in 124 days.

To Be Continued...

Victoria Santiago

My hobbies are drawing, eating, writing, and spending time with my cat. I live in Tennessee, which is known for country music.

Restored

"I shouldn't have taken the gem," Alia groaned, running through the broken buildings. She kept running into dead ends. "Uh-oh."

A week ago. Alia was in school thinking of random things until she got a great idea. *Wait, I have to make plan!* she thought before calling all of her friends together— all two of them.

"We came as fast as we could," said Miles, working to catch his breath.

"What's the plan?" asked Anora.

"The plan is sneak into the mayor's underground base," Alia announced.

"But no one has ever gotten into the base since it was built!" noted Miles, adding "Like the Coke vault, which is going to be impossible to get into for anybody."

Alia corrected him: "Impossible for one person, but not three."

Alia and her friends generally made a terrible team, but they still worked together to try and form a plan.

166

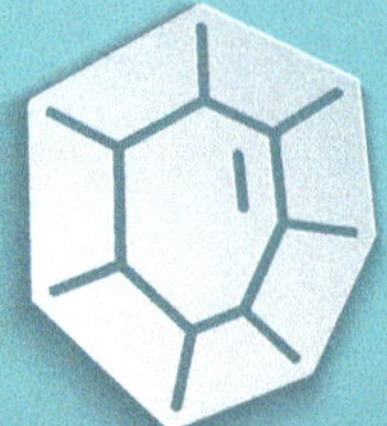

The next morning, Alia headed for the mayor's base with Miles and Anora in her ear. 12 grueling hours later, with a few breaks to nap and eat, Alia reached out over the walkie-talkies.

"I made it through. I actually made it. Through all of that. Miles, Anora, I'm in…"

"Wait, all three areas?" Miles asked enviously. "I've only gotten through the first!" He was still happy for her.

"Ok…any chance you guys can pick up the pace?" Anora asked nervously. "I think they're getting suspicious of me…"

"Miles, turn back," Alia ordered. "That's all the security they had. I'll just grab the gem and—" the buildings started to crumble right before her eyes, along with the gem. Alia was greeted by a black void before being woken.

"Alia, are you ok?" Anora asked, kneeling over her. The window next to Alia's desk at school was shattered; she was on the floor, and there was a rock lying on the ground beside her.

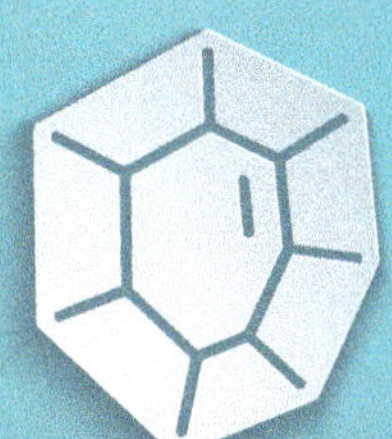

Las Personas son Estrellas

Poem

Las estrellas que puedes ver probablemente han desaparecido

Las estrellas son como las personas

Desaparecen sin que tú siquiera te des cuenta

Pero hay recordatorios de quién o qué pierdes

Las estrellas se van sin dejar rastro, pero la gente no

Familia o estrellas de lejos

No los ves, ni los escuchas hasta que se van

Las Personas son Estrellas: People Like Stars

Poem Translation

Stars you can see are most likely gone

The stars are just like people

They disappear without you even knowing

But there are reminders of who or what you lost

Stars leave without trace, but people don't

Family or stars from afar

You don't see, hear from them until they're gone.

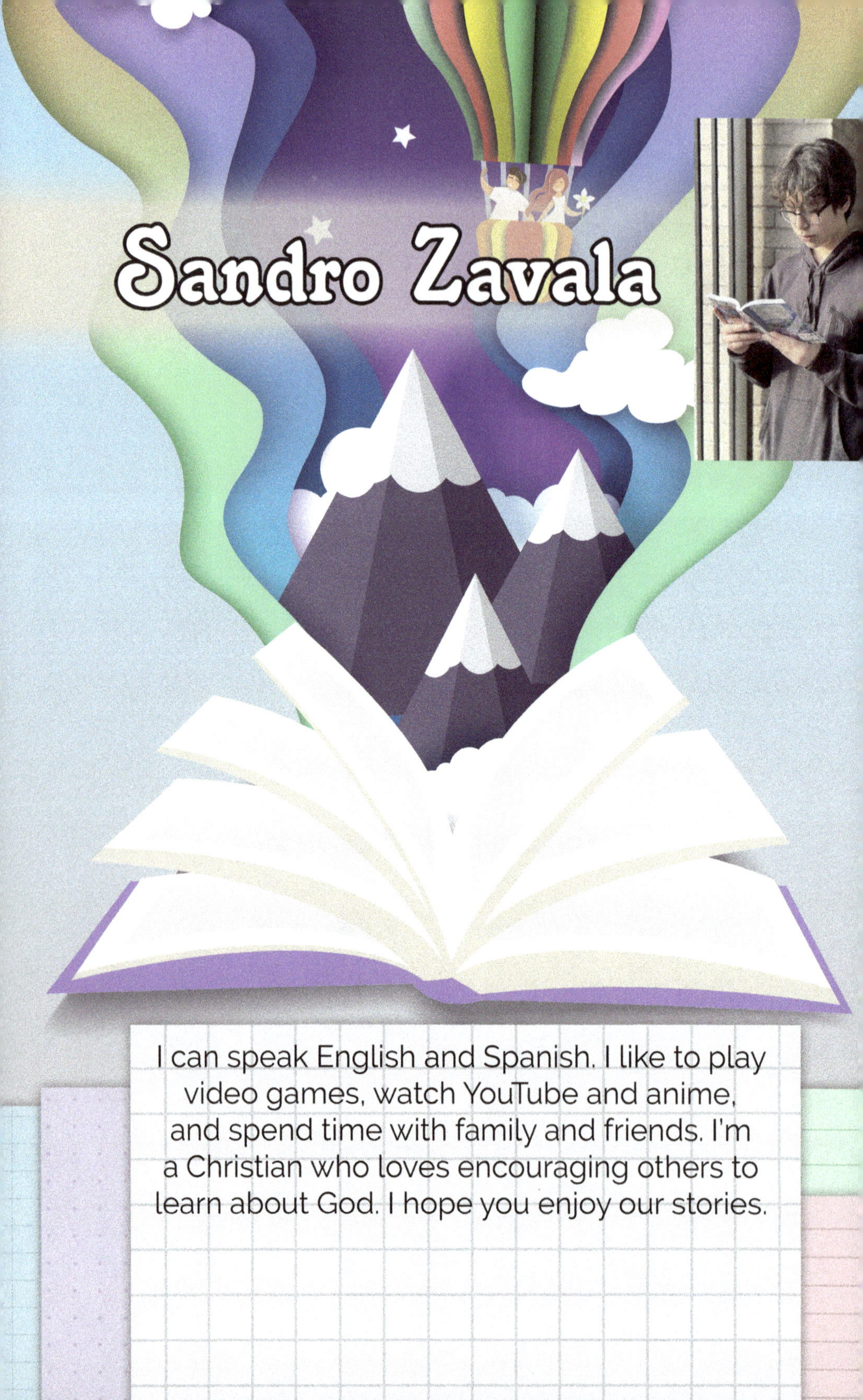

Sandro Zavala

I can speak English and Spanish. I like to play video games, watch YouTube and anime, and spend time with family and friends. I'm a Christian who loves encouraging others to learn about God. I hope you enjoy our stories.

THE LAST GUEST

Story Concept

Today, I woke up in a strange place. Last thing I could remember was taking the bacon leader with me using a grenade. I met new people; their names were Elliot, 007n7, Shedletsky, Chance, Noob, Builderman, Taph, Two Time, and Dusekkar. They told me that they too woke up here suddenly. We talked about what we all remembered.

Suddenly, we got teleported too somewhere random. There were generators and other people. When we went to meet them, they attacked. Turns out their names are Jason, c00lkidd, John Doe, Noli, and 1x1x1x1. They had special abilities and powers, but so did we.

We decided to divide into ranks. Sentinels and supports.

JORNADAS ESCOLARES Y AMIGOS

Lunes

Martes

Miércoles

Jueves

Viernes

estos son los días en que los niños son enviados a la escuela para "aprender"

pero lo único bueno es ver y pasar tiempo con tus amigos

además de eso, es pura tortura

hay algunos profesores que son aburridos y molestos

A veces hay bullies allí, pero no se les hace nada

Amigos son lo único que mantiene la escuela

Jornadas escolares y amigos: School Days and Friends

Poem Translation

Monday

Tuesday

Wednesday

Thursday

Friday

These are days children are sent to school to "learn," but the only good thing is seeing

and spending time with your friends.

Besides that, it's pure torture

There are some teachers who are boring and annoying.

Sometimes there are bullies there, but nothing is done about them

Friends are the only thing that keeps school bearable

Collaborative
Writing

Midnight in Hawthorn House

Collaborative Short Story
Written by Alyson and Victoria

The clock struck midnight and then stopped. A scream tore through the Hawthorn House. In the locked library, Mr. Hawthorn lay dead beside his desk. No windows were open. No one could have gotten in or out.

Detective Morris spotted unusual clues: ink stains on the victim's hands and a bitter-smelling teacup on the ground. As Detective Morris walked through the garden, he noticed the grass was wet, but no rain had been forecast.

Everyone had an alibi, but everyone was lying.

The detective returned to the library. On the desks was an unfinished will; all it needed was a signature. Mr. Hawthorne had planned to leave everything with Clara, according to her— from the looks of it, he changed his mind.

Then everything became clear.

Clara confronted her uncle in the garden earlier; she pleaded with him to change the will and choose her as the sole inheritance holder. She was angry and did the unthinkable: poisoned his tea and locked the door behind her. Clara had some string tricks up her sleeve to make it look like no one was ever there.

Detective Morris walked up to Clara and accused her of the crime, and she burst into tears. "I did not mean for it to happen. I thought I would teach him a lesson, not kill him," she whispered.

As the police led Clara away, the grandfather clock began to work again, right on time!

But the mansion would never feel the same.

Thanks
for
Reading!